Get down on your knees and beg forgiveness if you've got loads of money and you haven't done anything lately to help the poor. Jesus has just arrived on the East Coast to announce the Kingdom of God. He wants you to love God, love your neighbor, feed the hungry, clothe the naked, visit the imprisoned, welcome the stranger and console the downcast. The sooner the better because there's not much time left and you won't get to take your money with you into the Kingdom of God. That's for sure.

In *Jesus In America* you'll find many of the awesome miracles and parables that you loved as a child: the Good Samaritan, the Rich Fool, the Prodigal Son, the Rich Young Man, the Poor Widow, Lazarus the Paralytic and the Generous Publican. You'll see Jesus, God and Man, inviting the lowly to take the best seats at the banquet and presenting the rich with a stark choice: follow his teachings and enjoy eternal life or board the express to Gehenna.[1]

It's the same Jesus of Nazareth but he's lost the accent, stashed his halo and dressed for the times. He is as compassionate, righteous and confronted with temptation today as he was long ago: Jesus of the Gospels with fundamental news about the Kingdom of God for all Americans who have ears to hear with: "The last shall be first and the first shall be last."

---

1 Hell

Jesus in America

Jesus in America

MIRACLES AND PARABLES
OF HIS SECOND COMING

Brandon Philips

Copyright 2017 Brandon Philips, Hilo, HI 96720
All rights reserved.
e-book ISBN: 978-0-9857230-4-0
pbk ISBN-13: 9780985723057
ISBN-10: 098572305X

To all those who hunger and thirst for justice

Contents

CHAPTER 1

The Kingdom of God

"For what doth it profit a man, if he gain the whole world, and suffer the loss of his own soul? For the Son of man shall come in the glory of his Father with his angels and then he will render to every man according to his works."[2]

IN THE FOURTH YEAR OF the last President of the United States, there appeared in the sky a wondrous star that shone even during the day. In the afternoon of the Sabbath came a great gathering of clouds and a driving wind. Jesus, the Son of God, came in glory, clothed in a dazzling white robe. Four of the Apostles, Simon-Peter, Andrew, James and John, stood beside him. The trumpets of a host of angels

---

2 Matthew 16: 26-27 (D)

resounded and a chorus of hosannas rang out, announcing the Kingdom of God.[3] A thunderous voice from on high announced the arrival of God's Son who would now proclaim the Kingdom and the Day of Judgment. And so it happened on that day that Jesus arrived in Harvard Square in the little town of Cambridge, Massachusetts, which in those days was a seat of learning near Boston.

For a long time, no one in the multitudes about the square dared to move or make a sound. Traffic halted and drivers gaped at the amazing sight. Shortly, some of them awakened from their stupor and began to honk their horns. For they loved Jesus and knew by the signs that it was truly the Anointed One come from on high in glory. Pedestrians fell to their knees, praising God's name.

To the sound of celestial music, Jesus stepped off the cloud and set his feet on solid ground. He was five feet seven inches tall, of sturdy proportions and dark-bearded. His Apostles, all former fishermen from the Sea of Galilee, wore plain, homespun robes and sandals. They stood by Jesus, waiting for direction from him.

Jesus saw where he must go and said to them, "Follow me." And they walked from the place near a subway entrance to

---

3 Cf. John 1, 51 "Amen, amen, I say to you, you will see the heaven opened, and the angels of God ascending and descending upon the Son of man." (D)

the sidewalk across the street. There, at the gate of Harvard Yard, sat a paralytic, begging for alms. Passers-by had ignored his cries for mercy all day long. But as Jesus approached him, he cried out, "Lord Jesus, you've come back! Hallelujiah! Have mercy on me!" And Jesus reached into his robe and found a drachma. He gave the coin to the man and said gently to him, "Thou art cured. Rise and go home."[4]

The man immediately rose and leaped with joy, praising God in a loud voice. He asked Jesus, "Can I follow you?"

"No," said Jesus, "for I have an ecumenical conference to attend right now. Go get something to eat and then go tell all those whom you know that I have come again to judge mankind. Let them know that those who love God and keep his commandments shall be with me soon in the Kingdom of God." As multitudes pressed in upon him, Jesus said to the Apostles, "Let's get to the meeting." And they passed through a gate into Harvard Yard.

Under an elm tree, he halted and said to the Apostles, "This accursed race! Don't they have eyes to see with or ears to hear with? Can't they see that the paralytic out there on the sidewalk is one of the least of my brothers?" Then he turned and led them to the meeting.

---

4 Cf. Mark, 2:11 "I say to thee: Arise, take up thy bed, and go into thy house." (D)

That day, authorities of the world's great religions were meeting in an upstairs room. From the Far East came Zoroastrians, Sikhs, Buddhists and Hindus. From the Middle East came leaders of Judaism and Sunni and Shia Islam. And from Europe and America came Christian leaders and scholars of many denominations.

Jesus and his Apostles went in to meet them. And he was chosen to speak first, for he was more authoritative than all the others in the room. Simon-Peter handed him a scroll of the Prophet Isaiah to read from, and he stood and read: "…loose the bands of wickedness, undo the bundles that oppress, let them that are broken go free, and break asunder every burden. Deal thy bread to the hungry, and bring the needy and the harbourless into thy house: when thou shalt see one naked, cover him and despise not thy own flesh."[5] He raised his eyes for a moment at the men gathered around him in the room. Then he continued his reading, "The spirit of the Lord is upon me, because the Lord hath anointed me; he hath sent me to preach to the meek, to heal the contrite of heart, and to preach a release to the captives and deliverance to them that are shut up."[6] When he finished his reading, he handed the scroll back to Simon-Peter and sat down, saying, "I am the very fulfillment of the passage from the Old Testament that thou hast

5 Isaiah, 58: 6-7 (D)
6 Isaiah, 61: 1 (D)

just heard. This day my Father in Heaven has sent me to establish the Kingdom of God!"[7]

The scholars were bewildered and began to murmur. The Patriarch of Moscow asked him, "So, what are we supposed to do? Bow down and worship at your feet?"

"Thou must listen and hear the truth. This is why I have come again."

A Buddhist monk stood and asked him, "What exactly is this truth that you claim to speak?"

Jesus said in reply, "Amen, the Kingdom of God is here because I am here."

A Christian scholar rose and said in protest, "Are you all right? Who are you to make that claim?" Several sitting near him also rose in shock and disbelief, as the meaning of his words sank in.

Jesus waved his hand and said, "I know mine and mine know me. The Kingdom of God begins with me. It is open to the poor, the forgotten, the despised and all who live in lowly places. They will inherit all! Yes, the first will be last and the

---

7 Cf. Luke, 4: 21 "This day is fulfilled this scripture in your ears." (D)

last will be first. Oh, ye worse than senseless stones, thou who profess Christianity but ignore the Gospels and the Prophets."

At these words, some of the scholars rose and uttered curses against him, calling him the Son of the Evil One.

But again, he dismissed their clamor. "Yes, the truth I proclaim is that today's world order will be overthrown. It shall pass away but my words will not pass away![8] The wealthy and powerful will be cast down and the poor will rise over them. The least among thee—-the weak, the poor and the humble—-will go to the head of the table to enjoy my favor in the new Kingdom. This is the good news that I bring. Thou hast heard it here. Now, let the poor rejoice! The Kingdom of God is at hand."

The scholars were filled with fury and threatened to kill him.

Seeing their malice and their hardened hearts, Jesus stamped the dust from his sandals and gathered his Apostles around him to depart from that place. And they passed through their midst without harm.[9]

---

8 Luke, 21: 33 "Heaven and earth will pass away, but my words shall not pass away." (D)
9 Cf. Luke, 4: 30 But he, passing through the midst of them, went his way. (D)

CHAPTER 2

The Multitudes in Boston

"And when he said these things, all his adversaries were ashamed; and all the people rejoiced for all the things that were gloriously done by him."[10]

JESUS THEN LEFT HARVARD SQUARE, taking the MTA subway train to Park Square in downtown Boston. There, he led his Apostles to a grassy place near a fountain and began speaking to the crowds that gathered around him. Jesus raised his arms in blessing and cured them that had evil spirits. The blind saw, the deaf heard and the lame walked without crutches.

---

10 Luke, 13: 17 (D)

He taught them about the Kingdom of God and likened it to a harvest, promising that his angels would gather the weeds for burning and gather the grain for storage in the barn.[11]

Some of the scholars from the ecumenical conference who had rebuked him for blasphemy showed up in the crowd and accused him of violating the Sabbath. Jesus replied, "Do ye hypocrites never get out of bed on the Sabbath, take thy dog for a walk and pick up its excrement? Isn't that also breaking the Sabbath?"[12] His critics were shamed and the crowds rejoiced at Jesus's divine power over them.

Jesus and the Apostles left and walked towards South Station, passing through the financial district on the way. There, executives and moneychangers working on the weekend stared and laughed at their strange clothing and wild hair. These were men who set great store by the things of this world, and good hair above all other things except money, which they love most of all.

Jesus walked up three steps to the entrance of a large bank and began to preach. The Apostles stood near him so that he would not be crushed because throngs of workers and shoppers were pressing upon him. No sooner had he said

---

11 Cf. Matthew, 13: 30. "Gather up first the cockle, and bind it into bundles to burn, but the wheat gather ye into my barn." (D)

12 Based on Luke, 13: 15 "Ye hypocrites, doth not every one of you, on the Sabbath day, loose his ox or his ass from the manger, and lead them to water?" (D)

the words, "Blessed are the meek, for they…" than the Chief Executive of the bank, whose hair was impeccably groomed, came out and interrupted him. "Sorry, mister. You can't speak here on my steps. This is my building. I built it. You're trespassing on private property and interfering with our operations. You'll have to move along." Then he signaled to his guards.[13]

"Thou hast built it?" Jesus asked. "Show me thy hands." The Chief Executive refused to show him his hands. Jesus then said to him, "I will destroy this office building[14] and in three days I will raise up a new temple to glorify the Kingdom of God where the poor shall be welcome." At that, he waved his hand and changed the Chief Executive and his minions into humble street sweepers. The multitudes were astonished and said, "Who is this man that he has such power over Chief Executives?"

Jesus and the Apostles moved on but stopped again on their way to the train station. This time it was to deal with two arresting officers who were taking a woman into custody. She was loudly resisting efforts to put her into the back of a police car, crying out, "No, I won't get in the car. God only knows what you'll do to me." Jesus stepped

---

13 Cf. on John, 7: 32 "…the chief priests and the Pharisees sent guards to arrest him. (D)
14 Cf. Luke, 21: 6 "All that you see here—the days will come when there will not be a stone upon another stone that will not be thrown down." (D) Mark, 14: 58 "We heard him say, 'I will destroy this temple made with hands, and within three days I will build another not made with hands.'" (D)

forward and asked the police why the woman was being arrested. They said, "She's been caught in adultery." Jesus asked them, "Was she caught in the act alone?" He said this to test them. For he knew the score.

"No," they answered.

"Then, where is the one with whom she was caught? Why do ye not arrest him, too?" They were confused and had no answer for him. "Release her, I command thee," Jesus said. But they ignored him. He said to the two men, "There are some among thee who are not of pure heart and cause evil to those in their charge. Woe unto thee."

Simon-Peter handed him a piece of chalk and Jesus bent down and began to write things about them on the sidewalk. Soon, Jesus and the woman were alone, except for the Apostles. Jesus stood up and asked the woman, "Where are thy accusers?"

She said in reply, "I don't know, I guess you scared them off. Thank you so much. But who are you and why are you wearing such an outfit on a hot and humid day in Boston? And what's with the 'thee and thou' business?" Jesus told her that he was the Messiah and she seemed to understand. He added that she must change her ways and stay out of trouble.[15]

---

15 Cf. John, 8: 8-11 "...Then Jesus straightened up and said to her, "Woman, where are they that accused thee? Hath no man condemned thee? She replied, "No man, Lord." And Jesus said:

After that, he and the Apostles went to South Station, performing more miracles and gathering large crowds of people along the way.

Neither will I condemn thee. Go, and now sin no more." (D)

CHAPTER 3

Multiplication of Pizzas

THERE WERE FOUR THOUSAND PEOPLE following Jesus and the Apostles by the time they entered the large train station. James and John went on ahead to get tickets for New York City, while Jesus preached the good news of the Kingdom of God. When he finished, he blessed them and boarded the train. He took his seat while the disciples stowed their bags and found seats close by. Before the scheduled departure, he looked out the window at the throngs of downtrodden workers, the lame, the blind, the hungry, the poor and the ill and he was moved with pity for them. He turned to Simon-Peter in the seat next to him and said, "If I leave the least of my brothers like this, they will grow weak and will not be able to get home. We must feed them."

"But, how can we feed this many? We have little to give them and there is little food at the stands in the station. Besides, the train leaves soon."

Jesus said, "Tell me, what do we have on hand?"

Simon-Peter replied, "One anchovy pizza, one pepperoni pizza with mushrooms and olives and five submarine sand-wiches. You don't think…"

"Give them to me," Jesus said. Then, taking the sandwiches, he raised his eyes and said a blessing. Then he divided them and gave them back to the disciples. "Take these out to the people." He did the same with the pizzas and divided them, too. "Go now. Feed my flock!"[16] The disciples rushed from the train, staggering with food, and immediately had the throng sit down in groups of hundreds and fifties. There were so many of them that they covered the platform all the way from the track to the grand hall. They ate until they were full. Yet, there was enough for the Apostles to feed over four thousand people and still return with plenty left over.[17] The regular commuters in the station were astounded and said among themselves, "How did he do that? We've never seen anything like this before."[18]

---

16 Cf. John, 6: 11 "Jesus then took the loaves, gave thanks, and distributed them to those who were reclining and also as much of the fish as they wanted." (D) 1 Peter 5:2 "Feed the flock of God which is among you, taking care of it, not by constraint, but willingly, according to God: not for filthy lucre's sake, but voluntarily."

17 Cf. John, 6: 12-13 "And when they were filled, he said to his disciples: Gather up the fragments that remain, lest they be lost. They gathered up therefore, and filled twelve baskets with the fragments of the five barley loaves which remained over and above to them that had eaten." (D)

18 Cf. Mark, 2:12 "They were all amazed and glorified God saying, 'We have never seen anything like this.'" (A)

As the train pulled out of the station, Jesus waved to the multitudes and they waved back, singing and praising him to the skies. He turned to his disciples, shaking his head, and said, "I cannot believe that in a country with so many millionaires and billionaires, this many hungry, sick, poorly-clothed and homeless people could be roaming the streets. Sure, in the Dark Ages when the barbarians invaded Europe, we saw worse suffering. But that was then. This is now. And I realize even today, such a sight is common in third-world countries like Sudan and Burkina Faso—and I'm burning to deal with those countries. But dear God, Father in Heaven, something's very wrong here. This is the so-called greatest nation on earth! And some of its leaders actually boast that it is a Christian nation, established on Christian principles hundreds of years ago. Imagine! Christian principles! It's incredible the way they use my name. This generation does not follow my most important commandments, 'Love God and love thy neighbor'! I have seen them walk past the poor and the possessed here in the streets of Boston without even a glance! They seem heartless and without charity."

Simon-Peter replied to this outpouring with pointed praise for the basic goodness of Americans. "Master, the American people are generous. They have distributed immense treasure around the world. And besides that, every year they contribute tax money to their government to house the homeless and care for all kinds of needy people. They have a funny name for it. They call it welfare, not alms-giving, that's all."

"Oh, really? Is that all? This "welfare" takes care of all kinds of needy people? Then, do the possessed and the poorly-clothed people in the street not need help? Why are there still so many sick people begging and actually living in the streets? Thou hast seen them thyself. I hope we don't see any more of this in New York." Then Jesus rose and found another seat where he could be alone to meditate and pray.

CHAPTER 4

The Rich Young Man

"Jesus saith to him: If thou wilt be perfect, go sell what thou hast, and give to the poor, and thou shalt have treasure in heaven: and come follow me. And when the young man had heard this word, he went away sad: for he had great possessions."[19]

JESUS GOT OFF THE TRAIN with the Apostles at Union Station in New York and a large number of people came to him, reaching out to touch his cloak. After casting out demons and curing paralytics in the station, he withdrew quickly to Central Park and began to preach to the multitude. Andrew, James and John took up positions again to keep the people from crushing him. Meanwhile,

---

19 Matthew, 19: 22 (D)

Simon-Peter kept an eye out for the authorities, all the while wondering how he could tell Jesus that he must speak modern English.

A large number of millennials sat on the grass and listened to him teach about the coming of the Kingdom of God. And it happened that a young man who worked at a nearby hedge fund corporation passed by and heard Jesus speaking. At first he thought Jesus was a member of the Occupy Wall Street movement, but as he came closer, he was pleased to hear that Jesus was not stirring up class warfare but was offering salvation and everlasting life instead. He knelt down at the feet of Jesus and asked him, "Good Teacher, what must I do to live forever?"

Jesus said to him, "Thou hast to obey the commandments. No killing, no fudging on thy fiduciary responsibilities to clients, no worshipping the false god of Mammon[20], honor thy mother and father. This everyone knows."

The young man answered, "Yes! I know. I've been doing these things all my life, ever since I was a kid. So, will I have eternal life?"

---

20 A biblical term for money.

Jesus said in reply, "There's something else thou must do."

"Sure. Just tell me. Whatever it is, I'll do it," the young man said.

Jesus said to him, "Thou hast done very well in thy lifetime, keeping the commandments. And I love thee for that, but to have eternal life in the Kingdom of Heaven, thou must also take thy wealth and thy savings, and....by the way... how much dost thou make every year?"

"I'm not sure. A ton of money, I guess. Last year, I must have made three million dollars in salary and bonuses." He looked up in the air, "Yeah. At least that much. Maybe more. I haven't been keeping track. Why? Will it help?"

Jesus replied, "Not much. In fact, it may cause thee to lose thy soul. So, here's what thou must do. Go take what thou hast and give it away to the poor and, trust me, thou shalt receive thy treasure in heaven. Once thou hast done that, come and follow me as one of my apostles." Jesus looked at him closely and detected a look of disappointment. He changed his tone with the young man and said, "If thou dost not want to follow me like an apostle, then I say unto thee, give half thy fortune away." The crowd heard what he said to the young man and were overjoyed.

But, the young man's mouth fell open. His eyes widened in amazement. He stood before Jesus dumbstruck, as if he had suddenly got news of an IRS audit. Then he turned abruptly and walked away depressed, saying, "No way, man. No way."[21]

Jesus said to the multitude, "It is always a shock for the wealthy when they find out what they must do to enter the Kingdom of Heaven. For them, money is an addiction. They chase after money as if that is all there is in life. They lose regard for others. Some of them force workers into wage bondage and even withhold wages altogether from them. I have heard of many such cases just since my arrival."

A man in the crowd shouted, "That's right, Jesus. That happened to me and my buddies. Dozens of us. And the employer is a billionaire! The guy completely screwed us out of our wages."

Jesus said, "Amen, I say unto thee, thou can not be a money-grubber like that billionaire and claim to obey God's most important commandments. Is it not written that thou cannot worship both God and mammon?"[22]

---

21 Cf. Matthew, 19: 16-22 "...he went away sad for he had many possessions." (A)

22 Cf. Luke, 16: 13 "No servant can serve two masters: for either he will hate the one, and love the other; or he will hold on to the one, and despise the other. You cannot serve God and

Others in the crowd told Jesus they were living on subsistence wages, working long hours and still not able to provide for their families. And yet, their leaders were calling for tax breaks for the rich and the elimination of the minimum wage.

Jesus replied, "The rich will find it difficult to get through the gates of Heaven. In fact, it will be easier for a fat man to squeeze through one of these New York subway turnstiles than for a rich man to get into Heaven.[23] That young man who just left, sad to say, might not get in. I can't emphasize this enough. The last will be first and the first will be last.[24] Unless he repents and gives away most of his worldly possessions, he will likely end up being cast into the unquenchable fires where there will be wailing and the gnashing of teeth."

When Jesus finished speaking, Simon-Peter impatiently whispered to him, "Master, can I suggest something?"

Jesus replied, "Yes, what is it?"

---

mammon." (A)

23 Cf. Matthew, 19:24 "And again I say to you, it is easier for a camel to pass through the eye of a needle than for one who is rich to enter the kingdom of heaven." (A)

24 Matthew, 20: 16 (A)

"I've been listening to you all the time you've been speaking and I see the people struggling a bit with your language, your style."

"What is wrong with it?"

"It's a little, shall I say, hoary with age. Can't you tweak it, update it?"

Jesus rubbed his beard and nodded. "I will try."

Simon-Peter replied, "Good, terrific. Now, why don't we wrap it up and get out of here? I'd like to see what's happening over on Wall Street and what the Mammonites[25] are up to." So, he and the Apostles withdrew from the park amid great rejoicing at the good news Jesus had brought for the poor. But, the wealthy in the crowd left with great disappointment at the Master's teachings. For they had a lot of loot and decided that if they couldn't take it with them, they wanted no part of the Kingdom of Heaven.

---

25 A term for those devoted to the pursuit of money.

CHAPTER 5

Poor Lazarus

"And Abraham said to him: Son, remember that thou didst receive good things in thy lifetime, and likewise Lazareth evil things, but now he is comforted: and thou art tormented."[26]

IN A SHORT WHILE, THEY emerged from a subway tunnel and headed immediately for the great Houses of Mammon on Wall Street, the New York Stock Exchange, Goldman Sachs, Chase, Morgan Stanley and others. On the sidewalk they came before the brazen idol of the Mammonites, a life-size bull, posed in a headlong charge. Jesus and the disciples were shocked and outraged at this. The brothers, Andrew and John, both men of astonishing strength, put

---

26 Luke, 16: 25 (D)

their shoulders to the idol, trying to topple it. For was it not written that when Moses went up the mountain to talk to God, the Chosen People used his absence to fall to the ground and worship before a golden calf such as this? And weren't they punished severely when Moses returned and caused the idol to be destroyed? How was it at all possible that the people of a self-described Christian nation had fallen prey to such idolatry? Andrew and John struggled to topple the idol but grew exhausted. Simon-Peter said to them, "Give it up, boys. The pagans have gone to great length to secure their idol. It won't budge. Besides, the authorities are giving us stink-eye."

Jesus agreed with him and led his Apostles into the Stock Exchange. Once inside, he surveyed the scene and wished that he had a whip to apply to the backs of the idolaters. The devotees of Mammon got right in their faces and sneered. "What are you low-lifes doing in our holy of holies?" Hearing this, Simon-Peter lunged at one of them to knock some sense into him, but Jesus restrained him by the arm.

The Chief Executive signaled to security to hustle Jesus and his Apostles back onto the street, but Jesus raised his voice in authority, "I tell thee, I AM Back. And this time I mean business—-my kind of business. I gave you my Father's message two thousand years ago and thou didst not listen. Don't make the same mistake this time. Those who have ears will listen. The Kingdom of God is at hand.[27] I am the Light and the Way, sent by my Father. In a matter of days I will begin gathering up the faithful into the Kingdom of Heaven and cast sinners and the unjust into the dark. Amen, I tell you, thou cannot serve God and Mammon."

The moneychangers on the floor all began to throw crumpled-up orders at him and taunt him. "Mo-ney, mo-ney, mon-ey!" they chanted. "Show us the money if you are who you claim to be. Give us signs of your power." Before Jesus could say or do another thing, the Chief Executive and several armed officers came to Jesus and his disciples and surrounded them. Then, they led them into a nearby conference room. "This is too good," the Chief Executive said to Jesus, looking him up and down. "So, you are the Son of God?"

"Yes. You have said it, not I."

The leader of the secular pagan cult examined the strange clothing and the haloes above the heads of Jesus and his Apostles. He cautiously passed his hand through Jesus's halo but pulled it out quickly. "I don't know what tricks you've got up your sleeves, but let me tell you, we don't do Halloween parties here," he said, face to face with Jesus.

---

27 Cf. Matthew, 3:2; 4:17 (A)

Immediately, Simon-Peter pulled out a dagger and made a lunge to cut off the Chief Executive's ear, but again, Jesus restrained him.

"Damn right," said the executive, stepping away and alerting security. "Back off, you lousy bunch of clowns. I've heard all about you and that stupid nonsense in Boston. Second coming, a happy kingdom and all that rapture stuff. Let me tell you, I'm not playing."

Jesus looked at him and said, "Many will be called. But few will be chosen to enter the Kingdom of Heaven. And you are not one of the chosen." He turned to Simon-Peter and said, "Mark this man down for the express to Gehenna as soon as he shows up at the Pearly Gates."

Several security guards appeared and stood by. The executive snorted at Jesus, "What a joke! Wait right here while I go get a few friends to hear this. Don't go away." He had Jesus and the Apostles sit at a long table and soon returned with some of America's big money men and a few captains of industry. After they were seated, the Chief Executive said to Jesus, "Now, explain to them what you're doing here. I'm sure my friends from the world of mammon would all love to hear the good news about your mythical paradise. Is this all about some kind of Enchanted Kingdom in Florida?"

"I am the Light and the Way," Jesus said to the Chief Executive. "I'm here to tell you that the Kingdom of God is at hand. Be ready." The recently arrived men roared with laughter.

The Chief Executive taunted Jesus again. "How about letting us in on this sweet deal... this Kingdom of God?"

Jesus said to him, "First, sell your possessions and use the greater part of it to help the poor in your city. Then, the Kingdom will be yours."

"The greater part? Is that all?" the Chief Executive asked sarcastically. "You got to be crazy! We don't have that kind of loot to give away. We first have to satisfy all our stakeholders: our associates, myself, our CFO, our COO... and last of all, our investors." He threw a sly glance to his fellow-worshipers of Mammon.

Jesus exploded in anger and pounded the table, sliding back into his old English. "Thou hast failed to mention the poor! Let me tell thee a thing or two about thy stakeholders, ye den of thieves, ye brood of vipers, ye hypocrites! Woe unto thee, these last days before the judgment. Thou wilt face the coming wrath. Ye better forget thy hoard of cash, thy return on investment, thy yield curve, thy bundled derivatives, thy almighty p-e ratios! The angels are coming as we speak to separate the righteous from the wicked. Thou hast only a few days…"

The Chief Executive's face flushed. "Shut up! I've had enough of your nonsense and so have these gentlemen."

Jesus rose, saying in a loud voice, "You foul moneychangers, you devour the houses of widows and cover up your sins with financial mumbo-jumbo." Then he said to the Chief Executive, "Listen to me. You're the worst of sinners!"[28] His eyes bored into the soul of the executive, transfixing him as the other devotees of Mammon watched in silent astonishment. Simon Peter nodded with approval, seeing the effect that Jesus had on them.

Jesus then told this parable to them: "There was a CEO of a pharmaceutical company who dressed as you do, in the finest and most costly suits. Every day he went out for lunch to an expensive restaurant around the corner and ordered the choicest meats and the best wines. On his way to the restaurant one day, he saw a beggar, whose name was Lazarus, lying on a battered piece of cardboard on the sidewalk. The man's legs were covered with oozing sores. The CEO resented having to go out of his way to step around him. The poor man would have gladly eaten even

---

28 Cf. Luke, 20:47 "They devour the houses of widows and as a pretext they recite lengthy prayers. They will receive a very severe condemnation." (A)

the crumbs and measly scraps that fell from the table of the CEO, if only he were allowed. The rich man passed by him, went on to the restaurant and had a huge meal. After lunch, he headed back to his office building the way he came and saw that the beggar was gone. He inquired about him to an officer who replied, "You mean Lazarus? Oh, he just died a little while ago. His body has been taken to the morgue. Why do you ask? You got some business with him?"

"No, of course not," replied the CEO. And he thought that it served the beggar right for cluttering up the sidewalk. Then, he took the elevator up to his office on the 43rd floor but never got there because he had a major stroke in the elevator and collapsed and died. Whereupon, his soul flew down to the unquenchable flames of Gehenna. There, he felt his legs on fire and his mouth thirsting for even a drop of water. Looking up to heaven, he spied Father Abraham with Lazarus, sitting by his side, feasting on chicken and fries and sipping Red Bull. The CEO called out to Lazarus to be merciful and come down with his finger dipped in that drink to touch his parched tongue."

Jesus pointed a finger directly into the face of the Chief Executive as he continued. "Father Abraham told the rich man that he had had his turn living in luxury while poor Lazarus endured extreme misery on the streets. Now that the shoe was on the other foot, and Lazarus was enjoying his heavenly reward, justice was done. Abraham wished there was some way to help, but there was a big gulf now between them and there was simply no way to relieve the rich man's torment and suffering.

The rich man pleaded to Father Abraham, 'If you can't help me, at least give my friends and relatives a heads-up so they don't have to go through the same torture I am now in. Please, you must.'

Abraham told him. 'I don't think so. They never paid any attention to the message before, so what makes you think it'll be any different if we remind them again? Even if the prophets were to stand on their heads and chew figs or train camels to belly-dance, it wouldn't get their attention.'"[29]

When he finished the parable, Jesus looked at each of the moneychangers in the room and said, "Fair warning. I'm not doing this again. There will be no Third Coming. I'm tired of campaigning against greed. I'm telling you for your own salvation that it is better to give than to receive. Remember, your life and your possessions are two

---

29 Cf. Luke, 16:31 "And Abraham said to him: 'If they hear not Moses and the prophets, neither will they believe, if one rise again from the dead." (A)

different things.[30] Follow the example of the poor widow who, with her two coins donated proportionately more to charity than you do, though you are millionaires and billionaires.[31] You guys don't have a clue when it comes to generosity."[32]

But the men of mammon shook off their amazement at Jesus. They sneered and said, "Get the heck out of here." They rose as one, denouncing Jesus and threatening him with their fists.

"Repent!" cried Jesus.

"Socialist!" they shouted.

The Chief Executive signaled his guards and they swarmed around Jesus and the Apostles with guns drawn. As they tried to arrest Jesus, he raised his hand, halting them in their tracks. He looked up to Heaven and asked his heavenly Father, "Should I?"

---

30 Cf. Luke, 12:15 "Take heed and beware of all covetousness; for a man's life doth not consist in the abundance of things which he possesseth." (D)

31 Cf. Luke, 21: 1-4 "And looking on, he saw the rich men cast their gifts into the treasury. And he saw also a certain poor widow casting in two brass mites. And he said, 'Verily I say to you, that this poor widow hath cast in more than they all: For all these have of their abundance cast into the offerings of God: but she of her want, hath cast in all the living that she had" (D)

32 Cf. Luke, 6: 30 "Give to everyone who asks of you and from the one who takes what is yours do not demand it back." (A)

"Afraid so," said the Voice Above.

"Thy will be done," said Jesus. And looking at the Mammonites and their minions, he said, "A curse on this place of abominations!" And suddenly, they disappeared, replaced by piles of shiny, brass coins. Then, with a heavy heart, Jesus turned and said to the Apostles, "Let us go from this place. I really didn't intend this to happen."

Simon-Peter, patting him on the shoulder, said. "Don't feel bad, Jesus. They should have listened. You warned them. I heard it with my own ears."

Jesus said to him, "It was like this with the Pharisees back in the day in Jerusalem. They act like respectable professionals but basically, down deep, they're a greedy bunch. Where's the sense of morals or compassion today?"[33]

Andrew and John grabbed fistfuls of the brass coins on the way out of the conference room and as they left the House of Mammon, they flung them on the floor, touching off a scramble among the traders.

---

33 Cf. Luke, 16: 14-15 "The Pharisees, who loved money, heard all these things and sneered at him. And he said to them, "You justify yourselves in the sight of others, but God knows your hearts; for what is of human esteem is an abomination in the sight of God.'" (A)

CHAPTER 6

The One Percent

"And sighing deeply in spirit, he saith: Why
doth this generation seek a sign? Amen I
say to you, a sign shall not be given to this
generation."[34]

ON THE SIDEWALK OUTSIDE THE Stock Exchange, Jesus
sighed from the depths of his spirit and said to Simon-
Peter, "What a bummer."

Simon-Peter replied, "Nothing gets through the heads of
these millionaires and billionaires. Looks like the Second
Coming has hit a wall, at least as far as the one percent is
concerned."

---

34 Mark, 8: 12 (D)

"Yes, it's kind of depressing. And I fear there are plenty of others like them in this country. Got any ideas?" he asked the other Apostles.

Simon-Peter's brother, Andrew, suggested that Jesus might try his hand at some more awesome miracles on one of the city's main avenues. James said, "You need to sugar coat the message. How about opening a Broadway musical to push the good news?" John, the brother of James, said, "You could try leaping over a tall building. You never know. It might work." But Jesus nixed those ideas. He was finished with signs and miracles to prove who he was to the unbelievers. "Look, I'm done. Poke me with a fork. I've raised the dead. I've cured illnesses all the way from unclean spirits to withered hands and everything in between. You name it, I've done it. And I refuse to water down my teachings for them. The one percent are the worst. But I also worry about the poor, deluded millionaire wannabes up and down the social ladder."

Simon-Peter said to him, "Well, of course. Many of the one percent don't see anything in your message that they like. Just the opposite. They'll never give away the bulk of their money even if they're threatened with hell fire. So, the way I see it, Jesus, is we should concentrate on the one percent first and consider the options: One, just take their money, period. Delete all their accounts. That shouldn't be too hard for a Russian hacker worth his salt. Then watch them come around to seeing things your way. Two, we could modify our appearance. I mean, lose the beards, the woolen robes and the haloes and go get some Brooks Brothers suits. Dress for success! Then they might take us more seriously. Right now they look at us like we're in costume for a Hollywood epic like *Ben Hur* or *Exodus*. So, they don't even hear the message."

"What's the third option?" Jesus asked.

"Third, we cut our losses with the super-rich folks. Just drop them like a bad habit. After all, they're only one percent. They don't really count for much in the big picture. You should count your blessings that you've won over 99 percent!"

"I won't do that, Simon. I'm the Good Shepherd. I go out looking for stray sheep. That's my job. And besides, it's not just the rich. There are other pathetic strays out there that I just mentioned. The mixed-up, confused wannabes. There could be millions of them. Basically good people. They just need better leadership. I won't give up the search for them. I've got to keep trying to round up as many of them as I can, late as it is. Do you understand?"

"OK. Scratch option three. We don't give up on any of them. In that case, we need to try some combo of the other two: try and look more presentable while we put the squeeze on the very well-off. You know what, though? I still don't think it'll work. The minute you tell these people to give their money away, you'll lose them. You'll never get them into the last roundup. Not these people. Guaranteed."

"For crying out loud, I'm not telling them they have to go around wearing a hair shirt. They can keep all their stuff."

"What stuff you talking about?"

"You know, the mega-homes with movie theaters and bowling allies, infinity pools, personal jets, designer clothes, mud baths and so on. Whatever! I've got no problem with all that silly stuff. Just as long as they understand that I won't put up with wage slavery and sickening impoverishment for working people and obscene compensation packages for the super-rich. CEO's grabbing four or five hundred times what the average guy takes home. Golden parachutes worth hundreds of millions. It's shameful. Do you really understand what I'm saying, Simon?"

Simon-Peter replied, "I get it."

Jesus said to him, "So, that's my bottom line. And I mean it, because the billionaires don't see that their greed is crushing the little people. It's the age-old problem. What if you had to raise a family today on the minimum wage? So, listen. How about you getting together with Matthew up in Heaven, throw some figures together and see what you can come up with. I'll pitch the deal. If they can meet me halfway, I'll be satisfied. If not, then, I guess it'll have to be fire and brimstone for them."

Simon-Peter was pleased. "Will do. And, oh, by the way, what do you say about new clothes and haircuts for us?"

"Is it really as important as that?"

"Master, you don't know these people. They're nuts about hair. They spend hellaceous time and money on hair coloring, hair implants, hair grooming, hair styling, hair conditioners, and removing hair from the wrong places, and they show the same madness for grooming their dogs. The money involved is enough to feed half the starving people of the globe. As for clothes, please, don't get me started."

Jesus reflected a little and nodded. "Well, if we absolutely have to. But it's not fully in line with my message. Remember the parable of the lilies of the field?"

"Master, with all due respect. We're not plants. And by the way, I kind of like the new you."

"The new me?"

"Yes, the way you've been switching over from all this thee, thou, and thy stuff, blessed be this and blessed be that, gnashing teeth, unquenchable fires and so on. Duuuhhh. Folks today don't get it. Just keep on doing what you're doing."

"Great. Is that it for today?"

"I believe so," said Simon-Peter.

"Very good. Sufficient unto the day is the evil thereof. See you later."

Simon-Peter gnashed his teeth and left so that Jesus could get some rest for his weary head. He also needed to do an errand: get over to Radio City to prepare the way for Jesus to do an interview. It was time to broadcast a clear message to the Philistines of this generation.

CHAPTER 7

Blessed Are the Poor

"Then shall the king say to them that shall be on his right hand: 'Come, ye blessed of my Father, possess the kingdom prepared for you from the foundation of the world."[35]

A CERTAIN RADIO TALK-SHOW HOST welcomed Jesus on-air and went on and on about his garb and his halo. Jesus sat, unmoved by the chit-chat. The host said, "So, what you're doing is just incredible, with all those great signs and miracles in Boston and now here in New York. I've been following the conversation and I'd really like to have you bring the audience up to date on what exactly you're trying to accomplish. You've been talking about your Second

---

35 Matthew, 25: 33-41 (D)

Coming and a Kingdom of God, right? And by the way, what should I call you? Jesus? Messiah? Master?"

"Master will do. The reason I am here is to do what I promised long ago. It's pretty straightforward. I've come to proclaim the Kingdom of God and the Day of Judgment. I never fail to deliver on a promise even if it takes a few millennia."

"So, is it going well? Are you ready to wrap it all up pretty soon? Folks out there are getting kind of anxious."

"In the past few days I've addressed tens of thousands of believers. But some people of this generation reject me and do not believe. I tell you and all your listeners, I am the Son of God, the Messiah and the Good Shepherd."

The talk-show host replied, "Speaking of the Messiah, surely you know that lots of people over the years have claimed to be the Messiah. And I hate to say it but, as we speak, there are lots of folks right now in psychiatric wards here in New York who've got the Messiah complex. What do you say to the skeptics?"

Jesus said, "I grow more impatient every day with the skepticism and disbelief I encounter at every turn—mostly at higher echelons. A prophet is never honored in his own country. Even miracles fail to impress them."

"So, why have you waited so long, like two thousand years, to keep your promise? Why didn't you check your calendar and roll out the Kingdom of God sooner?"

Jesus nodded. "So, yes, it has been a long time. Maybe a little too long for you people. I realize that. But you see, a thousand years seems like only a day to me. I probably should have shortened the trial period a bit but my Father and I wanted to give humanity a good chance to redeem itself and embrace the truth."

"Which is....?"

"Which is that we must love God and our fellow man in order to enter the Kingdom of God."

"Hmm. Sounds simple. But the devil is in the details. And one of the worst of the details, from what I understand, is that we've got to share our wealth. You tell us the rich will not get into heaven unless they divest themselves of material wealth, give it to the poor and simply trust in God. Am I right?"

"It is as you say."

"More or less? Or strictly speaking?"

"My Father and I do not call upon the wealthy to go out into the desert and survive on locusts, bread and water, like John the Baptist did. But, all of us need to monitor ourselves and realize what is important and what is immaterial. Money isn't all there is to life."

"You constantly hammer away at avoiding greed."

"I do. It bears repeating. It's important to keep God's commandment, love thy neighbor, especially the poor. The rich have a disordered attachment to earthly treasure and a disregard for the treasure that awaits them in heaven. They can easily make do with a smaller fraction of what they own. In fact a tiny fraction may still be too much. Think, for example, of your biggest mercantile family. A mere one one-thousandth of their fortune comes to one hundred thirty million dollars."

The show host said, "We Americans don't care how much the rich make. They earned it. They should get to keep all they earn. There have to be incentives to get people to work. Here in America, we also believe in industriousness and a God in Heaven who blesses the industrious with wealth."

Jesus replied to him, "There is only one God that I know of and I'm here to tell you that there is no such thing as the Gospel of Prosperity. No such thing. It's an abomination."

"Master, I'm sorry. You're out of sync. You love the poor too much and you don't give the wealthy due respect. Why on earth did you create so many poor people?"

"God did not make the poor. Your oligarchs did. Poverty is institutional in this country, and backed by the powerful. You equate the 'pursuit of happiness' with amassing mindless and unholy extremes of money. You devote all your energy to making a living but you have no life. Amen, there is not a private fortune in this land that was made with my Father's blessing. He does not look down and smile on the rich. To think that he does is anti-Christian."

The radio host objected, saying, "The poor are not nice people. They're mostly sorry, lazy-ass bums. When I was growing up, I always heard that God helps those who help themselves."

Jesus replied sternly, "Your hearing is very selective. Let me say it again. I am THE spokesman for the downtrodden, the marginalized, the excluded, the foreign, the ill, the imprisoned, the despised, those left behind and forgotten. Amen, I tell you, read the Gospels to know on whose side I stand."

"You just hate and despise the rich!"

"The rich have their champions in the world of Mammon and in the highest governmental circles. They don't need me to speak for them. What they need is for me to liberate them from the power of Mammon. Have you ever heard me say, 'Blessed are the wealthy for they shall inherit the earth?' Where in the Gospels do you read, 'Do not be afraid, you of the upper class, for your Father is pleased to give you the kingdom?' Or, 'It is harder for a *poor* man to enter the Kingdom of Heaven than it is to pass through the eye of a needle.' You know very well from reading the Gospels the kind of people I used to hang out with back in the day—-repentant sinners, the poor, the tax collectors,[36] the handicapped, the lepers, the possessed. Lowly people! I cured them, I consoled them, I forgave them. In the Kingdom of God, the last will be first and the first last. My message is consistent, clear and simple to understand and always will be."

When Jesus finished, the host was both confused and angry. He said to Jesus, "Red-blooded Americans, true Americans don't want any part of your socialist agenda. It won't work. It's been tried before in Eastern Europe and Russia and Cuba and that was a big flop, you'll have to agree."

---

36 Cf. Luke, 5: 30-32 "But the Pharisees and scribes murmured, saying to his disciples: Why do you eat and drink with publicans and sinners?" (A)

Jesus replied, "When you institutionalize the repression of the poor, bad things happen—even to wealthy aristocrats. Europe's hereditary aristocracies have mostly passed away and America's financial elites—your aristocracy—will soon suffer the same fate. My concern is that they don't see the coming wrath."

The program stopped for a commercial break. For, even the Second Coming takes second place in America.

* * *

The program host resumed where the conversation had left off, "You're wrong. We don't have a hereditary class society."

"My Father and I see all, even into your heart at this moment."

The host stiffened his neck and declared, "You know what I think? You're calling for class warfare and you're stirring up the politics of envy. You're not the Son of God. God would not pit low income earners against the better off."

Jesus replied, "God hasn't ordained that mankind be organized into castes and outcastes."

"But it's a dog-eat-dog world out there. Only the strong survive. What you promote is to simply wipe out the best and the fittest, the ones at the top of the social ladder who got there through hard work and competition. The struggle to reach the top is what makes the world a better place."

Jesus let out a deep sigh. "From what you just said, you must believe in the theory of evolution. Yet some of you Americans denounce evolution as godless. Which would you have?"

The talk-show host felt flustered and confused by his conversation with Jesus and declared, "Look, the job-creators are the best and that's all I can say. So, let's move on. What's next on your provocative agenda, Jesus?"

"Baltimore is next and after that we go to Washington to begin separating the sheep from the goats. Remember, I'm for the sheep. They're coming with me."[37]

"Say no more. I get it. The goats will be heading for the fiery pit. Are you going to try and see the President when you get to Washington?"

"Of course."

---

37 Matthew, 25: 31-46 (A)

"What will you say to him IF you get a chance?"

"Oh, he'll see me all right. I'll tell him to repent. Obey the most important commandment—-love God and love others as he loves himself. A tall order for him."

"What if he doesn't see eye to eye with you?"

"I'll throw him down from his throne."

The program host laughed at that and said, "I think he's doing great."

"He does great things for the rich and little for the poor. He must repent and change."

"And let's say he does change his ways and does as you command, even at the last moment…?"

"He will be received into the Kingdom of God just like the late-arriving workers in the vineyard."

The host replied, "I just don't get that last part at all, but it's been great having you on the show. Thank you, Master." He turned to speak directly into the microphone and said, "Well, there you have it, folks. Our guest, the self-styled Jesus Christ and Son of God in Heaven, in person, now on his Second Coming tour along the East Coast and speaking to you from our studio. Will miracles never cease? The next stop for him and his Apostles will be Baltimore, followed by an appearance in Washington, D.C. He says that when he gets to Washington and sees the president, he might have to overthrow him. How that plays out we'll just have to wait and see. Should be exciting. And now a word from our sponsor. I'll be right back. Don't go away."

Jesus met his Apostles in the lobby of the building. "Let's hope the message gets out," he said. Then they left that place and went down to the station to catch the train to Baltimore.

CHAPTER 8

Do Unto Others

"Amen I say to you, as long as you did it not to one of these least, neither did you do it to me. And these shall go into everlasting punishment: but the just into everlasting life."[38]

LATER THAT DAY, AFTER ARRIVING in Baltimore, Jesus led his Apostles through the streets, drawing ever-greater crowds. The sight of so many flocking to hear his message made him happy. "They always do it for me," he said to Simon-Peter with a big smile on his face. "My kind of people, the least of my brothers—and sisters. And don't you ever ignore the sisters, or there will be hell to pay."

---

38 Matthew, 25: 44-46 (D)

As he moved among the multitudes, he touched and healed many who were sick and they leaped with joy. There were also some only recently released from jail, weary of the constant tribulations of joblessness and being broke. He heard their lamentations and was moved with pity for them. He doubled his consolations and promises of reward in the Kingdom of God.

Jesus came to a park and stood on a bench so that he could be heard. He taught the people, quoting the words of the prophets, and they were surprised by his message that they, not their overlords, would be the first to enter the Kingdom. He told of the judgment to come and the great welcome he had prepared for them. "For I was hungry and you gave me food, I was thirsty and you gave me drink, a stranger and you welcomed me, naked and you clothed me, ill and you cared for me, in prison and you visited me."

A young man stepped forward and said, "I don't remember doing those things for you, Jesus."

"My son, whenever you did anything for one of the brothers or sisters, you did the same for me. And for those who didn't give food, drink, shelter, welcome and comfort to those in need, I'm saying they failed to help me. They'll face severe punishment on the Day of Judgment and the righteous will receive their reward in eternal life. Amen."[39]

As Jesus stood there in the park and looked over the heads of the people, he saw uniformed authorities moving among them with their clubs in hand. Simon-Peter warned him that they were coming. Jesus did not wish to expose the flock to any risk. So, he closed quickly with a parable about a distant ruler and his disordered attachment to earthly treasure. When the authorities were almost upon him, he performed an amazing miracle with a wave of his hand. Where there was once a bail bond office across the street, there was now a Dunkin Donuts. Suddenly distracted by the aroma of donuts, the authorities hurried there.

Jesus then withdrew from the park and wandered among the poor in the streets. They swarmed around him lamenting their suffering, their poverty, their shabby clothes, the poor quality food, their ratty apartments. And he said, "My little ones, listen, you worry too much. Isn't your life more important than all those things? Look at the birds. They don't work, and yet your heavenly Father feeds them. Aren't you more important to Him than they are? All the worrying in the world won't add a single minute to your lifespan.[40]

---

39 Cf. Matthew, 25, 31-46
40 Cf. Matthew, 6:24-34 "…Is not the life more than the meat: and the body more than the raiment? Behold the birds of the air, for they neither sow, nor do they reap, nor gather into barns: and

And why worry about clothes? Look at the flowers—-even royalty can't match their beauty. Bah, that's the kind of stuff that pagans seek. Besides, you wouldn't be caught dead in some of the clothes they're selling today. They look like rags to begin with, like those designer jeans, all ripped at the knees and bleached-out. They should pay you to wear them! Amen! You must first seek the kingdom of God and his righteousness, and he'll take care of all the rest for you. Don't worry about tomorrow. Tomorrow will take care of itself. Sufficient unto the day is the evil thereof."[41]

The people looked puzzled at his last words. Simon-Peter leaned towards him and whispered, "I keep telling you about that antiquated talk."

Jesus nodded and turned to the people again, "Folks, you heard me. Take it a day at a time. Each and every day of your life you've got enough to handle. So, chill. Relax, baby. You're in good hands—God's hands." He turned to Simon-Peter, "How's that for plain talk?"

"That's more like it but just look at them. They're as hungry as that bunch in Boston. Looks to me like they could

---

your heavenly Father feeds them." (D)
41 Matthew, 6: 34 "Be not therefore solicitous for tomorrow; for the morrow will be solicitous for itself. Sufficient unto the day is the evil thereof." (D)

all do with a good meal. How about fixing something right now for them?"

"You're right. I've got to feed my flock. And burgers and fries just won't suffice." He instructed the Apostles to go around the corner where they would find four catering trucks waiting for them and bring them to him. In the meantime, he would set up the tents and tables. Immediately, after the Apostles left for the food, a large tent arose in the park and the multitude surged forth. The Apostles returned and placed vast quantities of fresh, nutritious vegetable dishes and salads on the tables. There were also platters heaped with fish and meat and unimaginable quantities of apples, oranges, bananas, pineapples and, of course, Medjool dates—-Jesus's favorite dessert. TV news reporters caught the whole scene for the evening programs.

The crowds were amazed when they saw these things, for not in living memory had they seen so much fresh, wholesome food. The Apostles even distributed large bags to them so that they could take all they could carry home with them. The people exclaimed that all these things seemed utterly impossible. And Jesus said to them, "All things are possible to those who have faith. From now on, the first shall eat at Seven Eleven and the last shall dine at the Ritz Carlton!" The crowd cried hosannas to him until darkness fell and they went home.

CHAPTER 9

How to Pray

> "Therefore when thou dost an almsdeed, sound
> not a trumpet before thee, as the hypocrites
> do in the synagogues and the streets, that they
> may be honored by men...But thou when thou
> shalt pray, enter into thy chamber, and having
> shut the door, pray to thy Father in secret."[42]

JESUS WITHDREW FROM THE PARK and found lodging at an inn. To a crowd that suddenly gathered there he called out a window and said to those below, "The Kingdom of God is at hand. Be ready and pray to God with a pure heart. For, the hypocrites will try to lead you astray. Theirs is not the message of God. Do not follow the example of those TV preachers, who strut and shout or sit on those golden

---

42 Matthew, 6: 2-6 (D)

thrones, making a big show of their holiness.[43] That's not what my Father in Heaven teaches. Instead, when the Kingdom of God comes, you must go into your bedroom and close the door so no one can see you pray in secrecy to your Father. No need to make a big scene and get all melodramatic. He already knows what you need."[44]

He was moved with pity for the people in the crowd who had walked so far. He urged them, saying, "Keep your chins up. I'm leaving you for a while but I thank you all out there. Thank you for receiving me so warmly in your city. You shall be with me in the Kingdom of Heaven. I promise. Heaven is waiting for you. In the Kingdom of God you'll never go hungry again at our round-the-clock buffets. And you'll never shed another tear, either. In the Kingdom of God you'll be laughing your butt off, not crying your heart out."[45] Simon-Peter, who was standing next to him, raised his eyebrows. Jesus then raised his hand and blessed the multitude before closing the window.

Simon-Peter asked Jesus, "What was that all about?"

---

43 Cf. Matthew, 23: 6, "And they love the first places at feasts, and the first chairs in the synagogues." (D)

44 Cf. Matthew, 6: 6

45 Cf. Luke, 6: 21 "Blessed are ye that weep now: for you shall laugh." (A)

"Just a last-minute pep talk. There are lots of sheep in the flock that could go wobbly. Things might get scary for them in the countdown when I have to deal with the powers that be. I want to see that all my lambs come home safely on the big day." He drew the curtains and said, "Whew, I'm bushed. What's up tomorrow?"

"Haircuts and shaves. And new suits."

Jesus said, "So be it," and then he turned in for the night.

CHAPTER 10

The Clip Joint

"I have seen all things that are done under the sun and behold all is vanity"[46]

THE NEXT MORNING JESUS AND the Apostles found a shop where they could get their hair cut and their beards shaved in the manner of the locals. For, in recent days, Simon-Peter had been constantly bugging Jesus to go for a new look. They entered the shop and were immediately received by the owner, the son of Italian immigrants. Within minutes there were mounds of dark hair on the floor. And the faces of Jesus and his Apostles shone radiantly.

---

46 Ecclesiastes, 1:14 (D)

The barber, a certain Giovanni Bautisto, cut Simon-Peter's hair last. He asked Simon-Peter where he came from and he replied, "The Sea of Galilee." The barber had not heard of that place.

"Also known as Lake Tiberias," Simon-Peter added.

"Is that in Maryland?" Giovanni asked. Simon-Peter replied that he did not believe so, for he had never heard of that place either. "It's somewhere in what you call the Middle East, I think."

Giovanni gave him a nervous look. "Damn. That's a terrible place. All those bombings and killings. You ain't one of those terrorists, are you?"

"You have no reason to fear," said Simon-Peter.

"You guys Democrats or Republicans?"

"We are not Publicans," replied Simon-Peter. "Though, there are some among them whom we admire, because they're willing to help the least of our brothers."[47]

---

47 Cf. Luke, 19: 8 "But Zacchaeus standing, said to the Lord, "Behold, Lord, the half of my goods I give to the poor and if I have wronged any man of anything, I restore him fourfold." (D)

Giovanni scratched his head at that answer. "So, what do you guys do?"

Simon-Peter answered in reply, "Well, that's Jesus over there. He's the Messiah and we're his Apostles."

"You actors or something?" he asked, because he did not yet understand who they were.

"No, sir. Me and my brother Andrew are fishermen. So are James and John. It's hard work. And Jesus, there, he's a carpenter. But we're not in those lines of work anymore."

Giovanni asked, "So, what do you do now? You work in the fields picking crops?"

"No, we work among the poor."

"Sounds like a waste of time to me, but hey, it's none of my business. What do you think of our President? He's like us—-got the common touch. You'd never know he's a billionaire."

"It's funny you ask. We expect to see him a few days from now and Jesus will make up his mind what's to be done with him at that time."

"Really? You mean you're actually gonna see the President? Amazing. You guys don't look like the type that would get an invitation to the White House."

"We don't need an invitation. If ever we need to force our way into any situation, we call in our legions. Actually, though, it's looking to us like it's the other way around. The President's the one who probably won't get an invitation when the time comes."

The barber scratched his head again, not quite able to figure Simon-Peter out, thinking that all foreigners were a little weird. Then, finishing with Simon-Peter, he said, "OK. You're all done. That'll be twenty dollars apiece."

"One-hundred dollars?" Simon-Peter asked, as he reached deep into his pocket for some money.

Giovanni nodded. "Yeah. Tip's included and thanks for your business today. It's been a pleasure. Oh, by the way, I've been cutting hair here for thirty years and you guys are the first Messiahs and Apostles we've ever seen in here."

"I wouldn't be surprised, with the prices you charge," said Simon as he handed the barber what money he had.

"What's this?" Giovanni cried.

"It's all we have. And, tell me, is there a place around here, not too expensive, where we could go get some new clothes?"

The barber wanted to throw them all out, including Jesus, but stopped, seeing the halo glowing extra brilliantly about Jesus's head. It finally hit him. "Hey, wait a minute. Are you the guys I've seen on TV performing amazing tricks?"

"They're not tricks. Jesus is God. He can do anything he wants to."

Giovanni was amazed. "Oh, my God. I didn't realize. I should have known. Your robes...and those lights around your heads...." The barber fell to his knees. "Good God Almighty!" he exclaimed, crossing himself. "My apologies...there's no charge for you guys. It's on the house." He quickly stood up and asked if he could get his picture taken with them.

At that, Jesus put down an old magazine he was reading, and got everyone lined up for a selfie. Then he told the barber, "You should be more charitable with foreign people. Your own people have only recently arrived in this land.

Your xenophobia is forgiven. Now, once again, where can we get some decent clothes?"

Giovanni recommended the Salvation Army store for its low prices, just a few blocks down the street. Jesus and the Apostles thanked him and left the shop, happy with their new look.

CHAPTER 11

The Prodigal Son

"Son, thou art always with me, and all I have is thine...thy brother was dead and is come to life again; he was lost, and is found."[48]

WORD HAD GOTTEN OUT THAT Jesus was becoming popular among the masses not only in Baltimore, but also throughout the northeast. The wondrous news of his Kingdom also began to spread to Pennsylvania, Ohio, Indiana, Kentucky, Virginia and Tennessee. And busloads of believers converged suddenly on the city.

The authorities and the Mammonites grew nervous and wanted to bring his appearances in Baltimore to an end, but it was hopeless. In their desperation, they reached

---

48 Luke, 15: 31 (D)

out to Jesus and invited him to speak at a special meeting of the Chamber of Commerce, hoping to co-opt his
movement. Jesus agreed to attend and give a talk, for he
was impressed with what progress had been made in the
material condition of mankind over the centuries, thanks
to men of science, business, commerce, agriculture and
finance. True, the peasants and the laborers had done
the actual, backbreaking toil down through the years but
sharp minds provided the spark and the direction. And
he hoped that he could enlist such people in the launch-
ing of the Kingdom of God. He knew from Simon-Peter's
discussions with Matthew that it was time to modify his
methods.

But would the members of the Chamber buy into his
over-all plan, he wondered? Simon-Peter's views on the
inseparability of the rich from their money bothered him.

Jesus and the Apostles entered the hall with their physical
appearance greatly changed. They had stashed their haloes.
They had shed their woolen robes for dignified suits and
ties. And with their haircuts, they were almost indistin-
guishable from their hosts. Simon-Peter even sported a
gleaming watch. The Chamber president complimented
them on their new look but asked them what they had
done with their haloes, so widely remarked upon in news

coverage. Jesus said to him, "We needed to get with the program."

The Chamber laid out a sumptuous feast that was perfect except for one minor detail: they ran out of wine. Simon-Peter told Jesus of their hosts' problem and he said, "Let me take care of it."

The Chamber President had no idea what could be done. But Jesus ordered the busboys to fill the old wine bottles with water and bring them back from the kitchen. Miraculously, when placed on the tables, the bottles were again full of wine. The sommelier even remarked that it was superior to the wine that had been consumed earlier.[49] The party resumed without missing a beat and Jesus knew that he had scored with the well-heeled crowd.

After the feast, Jesus was led to a hall and was introduced to a large audience. He thanked them for their invitation and asked if they would agree to a simple question-and-answer program rather than a long-winded speech. For the most part the questions were respectful until a banker rose and asked, "Teacher, which is better, to raise taxes on the job creators or to improve living conditions for the poor? For

---

49 Cf. John, 2: 9 "And when the chief steward tasted the water made wine, and knew not whence it was, but the waiters knew who had drawn the water; the chief steward calleth the bridegroom and saith to him... 'thou hast kept the good wine until now.'" (D)

you cannot have both at the same time. When taxes rise, job creators do not hire." His question was meant to test Jesus.

Jesus saw what was in the banker's heart and he knew that his success or failure with the Chamber depended on a good answer. It was clear that low-paid workers had not caused the recent recession and that the desire for quick profits in the world of high finance was the root evil. In fact, the banker himself had a history of foreclosing on some homes that did not even have mortgages with his bank. Among such victims of fraud were widows and orphans.

Jesus said to him, "Workers and job creators have many interests in common. Managing for short-term profit often obscures this. Let me explain this with a business-friendly parable."

The audience of businessmen and women listened closely. And Jesus said to them, "There was a young man who worked in his father's moderately profitable towing business in Akron, Ohio. But he grew unhappy with his life, even though he was prospering and was able to bank much of his earnings. He felt oppressed living in his father's house and yearned for quicker riches and more fun elsewhere. So, he went to his father and told him that he wanted to move to Vegas where he heard there were great opportunities in real estate.

His father pleaded with him not to leave but to stay and continue working alongside his brother and fellow workers with the assurance that some day the business would be bigger and everyone would have a share in it. For his father was only too happy to reward hard work by sharing the wealth. What need did he have to take a thousand times as much pay as the workers, keeping them in penury?

The young man refused to listen. He went to the bank and withdrew all his savings, took his inheritance, bought a new car and left home to the weeping and wailing of his parents. He arrived after several days in the arid land of Nevada and took a job with a real estate firm. He was a talkative, sociable fellow and had the perfect personality for working with clients. He sold dozens of homes to wealthy people as well as to those who had no real prospect of making their mortgage payments. Soon, he was making tons of money. With his riches accumulating, he attracted lots of friends. He bought a palatial home, hired a chauffeur, stuffed his walk-in closets with new clothes and hosted parties around the infinity pool. He gambled away huge amounts of money at the casinos. And never once did he regret leaving his old life in Ohio behind.[50]

---

50 Cf. Luke, 15: 12

Then there occurred a terrible real estate meltdown caused by corrupt moneylenders and agents like him. Property values in Las Vegas suddenly crashed. Thousands lost their homes and values were cut in half and half again. Widows and other single moms with children were especially hit hard. The young man's cash flow dried up and he could not make his payments. He held no more parties. He sold his car. He let his chauffeur go. He sold the furniture and, when things got even tighter, he cleaned out the closets. Finally he sold his home on the hill overlooking the city. He lost his job and did any kind of work he could find. Naturally he saw no more of his friends.[51]

Time passed. Life took him eventually to the bottom of society—-among the outcastes and immigrants, the despised, the poor and the wretched. As his life drifted downward, he found living space under a highway overpass. He washed dishes and hauled out garbage at a hotel ten hours or more a day. He secretly picked over dirty dishes for morsels of meat or fish. His boss constantly harangued him to work harder or be let go. He lost his insurance coverage just when his health began to tank and in despair, he cried out to God, 'Why me?' And he pined for the life that

---

51 Cf. Luke, 15: 12-13 "and the younger son said to his father, 'Father, give me the portion of substance that falleth to me. And he divided unto them his substance. And not many days after, the younger son, gathering all together, went abroad into a far country: and there wasted his substance living riotously."(D)

he had once lived in Ohio, remembering that his father treated all people kindly and looked after the welfare of all of his workers and their families. He decided to return home even if it meant taking the most menial job in the family business.

As he drew close to his father's tow truck yard, he could see that in his absence, the business had grown greatly. His brother and father were out giving directions to dozens of productive, happy employees. His father and his brother looked confident and content with their roles. He was overcome with remorse and exhaustion from his journey and almost fainted dead away.

Then, his father caught sight of him. Seeing him dressed in rags and looking gaunt and pale, he wept. He ran to him and embraced him, calling out to the elder son in the yard, 'Hurry, let's get him inside and get him cleaned up.' With great affection he took care of his son's immediate needs. He had his older son organize a big feast. The older son chafed at this, and resented that his prodigal brother was to be treated so well. His father had done nothing like that for him. 'Why are you doing this, Dad?' he asked. 'You never held a big party for me, and yet I have been here all along, day in day out, doing whatever it took, working on grimy truck engines, sweating in the heat, dealing with customer complaints. When did you ever reward me?'

'Son,' he said, 'It's true you've been here with me all along and indeed you haven't behaved badly or cheated anyone, as your brother has. But he lost his way in the desert believing that life was all about chasing a fast buck. He worshiped false gods but has now returned to the fold.'"[52]

When he finished the parable, Jesus paused. Then he said. "Gentlemen, it is good to aim for material improvement in life, but the frantic, unrestrained pursuit of money is evil and leads to crimes against innocent lambs. Beware of the fast-buck fool! He will wreck the economy and cause untold misery. Is it not written, 'Thou shalt not kill the goose that lays the golden egg?' Think instead of long-term profitability and common interests that you have with all your stakeholders, including your low-income employees and your neighbors. You will reap more dividends in the end."

Some members of the Chamber stood and gave Jesus a long, standing ovation, for they shared his views. Jesus was amazed and smiled modestly. He had hoped for such a miracle but wasn't sure it would happen. He was also happy that Simon-Peter had pushed the issue of proper business attire with him.

---

52 Cf. Luke, 15: 11-32.

Behind the stage, Simon-Peter and the boys bunched their fists and raised them aloft. When Jesus came back and joined them, they all went off to a nearby inn and celebrated their success over many bottles of good wine.

CHAPTER 12

The Good Shepherd

"When did we see thee a stranger and took thee in or naked and covered thee?"[53]

THE NEXT DAY JESUS AND the boys walked to downtown Baltimore to visit the Good Shepherd Mission House. Neither Jesus nor the Apostles were very perky, given the amount of wine they had put away the night before. Even if you are a combo of God and the Son of Man, you don't get off entirely scot-free.

There was a long line of poor men, women and children waiting outside the two-story building. Jesus saw that a great banquet was about to be served and that the people who were invited were very hungry and impatient. The hall

---

53 **Matthew, 25: 38 (D)**

was crowded and noisy with those who had arrived first. Children were crying. Scuffles eventually broke out.

The good servants of the mission invited Jesus into the hall to meet with the chief steward. The Apostles followed them but went off to help the staff serve meals. Jesus was pleasantly surprised to see the kinds of people invited to this banquet. He said to the steward, "You have done well. I see that when you serve meals, you don't invite just your friends and relatives or the wealthy just to be sure of getting an invitation from them. You have invited refugees, the poor, the disabled—and you don't take a dime from them. I am pleased. I bless you."[54]

The chief steward replied, "Lord, I am not worthy that you should come to the Mission. Nor do I deserve special praise for not inviting the wealthy here at the Mission. The fact is they wouldn't accept our invitations anyway. Same is true of many of my own friends and relatives. They fear the poor."

Jesus then walked around the hall, meeting the people. A poor woman with two children approached him, weeping. She said to him, "If it wasn't for this mission house, my children and I would be starving to death. My husband died

---

54 Cf. Luke, 14: 13-14 "But when thou makest a dinner or supper, call not thy friends, nor thy brethren, nor thy kinsmen, nor thy neighbors who are rich...but when thou makes a feast, call the poor, the maimed, the lame and the blind." (D)

from working in the coalmines. I look for work but it's difficult with the children. What will happen to us? I'm so afraid of the future I can't sleep." Jesus reached behind her ear and plucked three gold coins out of thin air and gave them to her. He said to her, "Very soon the needs of your family will be taken care of in the Kingdom of God.[55] My peace I give you."

Everyone he passed in the hall tried to touch him knowing that he had the power to heal.[56] He came to a man wearing torn and dirty clothes that someone else had shared with him long ago. The man rose, took his hand and kissed it because he knew the power Jesus had. He said, "I thought this day would never come. I hear your words and I believe. You are the One sent by God."

Jesus said to all the others standing around him, "I will remind you of what John the Baptist said, 'Whoever has two cloaks should share with the person who has none. And whoever has food should do likewise.'[57] I say to those who have ears, go immediately to your closets and clean out everything you no longer need. Do the same with your storage lockers that are crammed to overflowing. Sell the contents and give the money to the poor."

---

55 Cf. Luke, 6:20 "Blessed are ye poor, for yours is the Kingdom of God. (D)
56 Cf. Luke, 6: 19 "And the multitude sought to touch him, for virtue went out from him, and healed all." (D)
57 Cf. Luke, 3: 11 "He that hath two coats, let him give to him that hath none; and he that hath meat, let him do in like manner." (D)

As he approached a little family in one corner of the room, he heard a Guatemalan man speaking Spanish. The man told him that he, his wife and two children had fled certain death in their country. A gang of youths had attacked his home with machetes and robbed them as they had dozens of others. The family fled and made a long and difficult journey through Mexico to come to this country. Yet, the man feared that all of them would be deported and face certain death in their homeland.

Jesus reassured him, "In the Kingdom of God strangers will be made welcome.[58] You will not be excluded but accepted with love, especially those of you who face violence and persecution in your own country."[59] He was stirred to pity over the harsh difficulty facing this family. "On the Day of Judgment, there will be weeping and wailing among those who raise barriers to keep out foreigners. They call themselves Christian but inside they are full of malice and spite. What good is it that they love their family and friends? It is not enough! Even sinners love their families and friends. There's no credit in that.[60] Amen, I say. The Kingdom of

---

58 Cf. Matthew, 25: 35 "For I was hungry and you gave me to eat; I was thirsty, and you gave me to drink; I was a stranger and you took me in." (A)

59 Based on Luke, 6: 20-26 "Blessed shall you be when men shall hate you, and when they shall separate you, and shall reproach you.... Be glad in that day and rejoice; for behold, your reward is great in heaven."

60 Cf. Luke, 6:31-33 "And as you would that men should do to you, do you also to them in like manner. And if you love them that love you, what thanks are to you? For sinners also love those that love them." (D)

God is not for such hypocrites. They do not follow my Father in Heaven who loves all. What is it that they don't they understand about the word 'all'?" Jesus left the man and his family telling them, "Have courage. Your Father will take care of your needs."

Jesus spoke to the whole multitude assembled in the room, "My children, I've seen your suffering and I've heard your sorrows but I bring you a message of hope. I have come to overturn the world order! A day of reckoning is coming, and on that day, you will jump with joy. The powers that be will face the wrath![61]

Jesus surveyed the room now lit up with beaming faces. "And on that happy day, you will inherit the kingdom. As for those who now rule over you? How will my Father receive them? I say, woe unto them. It would be better for them if they had not been born."

Jesus had them sit on the floor to listen to a parable. "There was a rich fool whose fields yielded great harvests. He had so much grain that he decided to tear down his barns and build larger ones to store it all, like those of this generation

---

61 Cf. Luke, 12:49-51 "I have come to set the earth on fire, and how I wish it were already blazing! There is a baptism with which I must be baptized, and how great is my anguish until it is accomplished. Do you think that I have come to establish peace on earth? No, I tell you, but rather division." (A)

who demolish their beautiful mansions only to build bigger ones. His sole purpose in life was to enjoy his wealth alone. But that very night, God told him that he was foolish to think that he would live to enjoy it all. Yes, he was wealthy in the things of this world—-but not for long and not by God's standards. That night, the foolish man died and God called him to account for his life on earth. Within a year, others who had inherited from him spent his entire hard-earned fortune.[62] I tell you, my children, this is what happens to those who hoard wealth for themselves but lack what matters most to God."

The multitude rejoiced at these words and leaped with happiness. He quieted them and said this before leaving the mission, "It is written, 'Therefore, do not be afraid anymore, little flock, because your Father is pleased to give you the kingdom.'"[63]

Simon-Peter looked at his watch and whispered to Jesus, "Lord, we better get moving. We've only got a half-hour to catch the train to D.C." And they hastily left for the station.

---

[62] Cf. Luke, 12: 20-21. "You fool, this night your life will be demanded of you; and the things that you have prepared, to whom will they belong?" Thus it will be for the one who stores up treasure for himself but is not rich in what matters to God." (D)

[63] Luke 12: 32 "Fear not, little flock, for it hath pleased your Father to give you a kingdom." (A)

CHAPTER 13

For All God's Children

A CERTAIN WEALTHY MERCHANT FROM California had seen coverage of Jesus's miracles in Boston and New York. He had also heard the messages of hope for the Kingdom of God that Jesus proclaimed to the multitudes in Baltimore. And he desired greatly to see Jesus in person. From the grand hotel where he was staying in Washington, D.C. he sent a servant to Jesus and the Apostles to invite them to a special gathering.

The merchant was a pious Christian and a philanthropist who donated to Church causes. On this occasion at the hotel he was sponsoring an exclusive three-day conference for Christian clergy, wealthy laymen and influential Washington insiders. The conference featured various lectures, seminars, wine and cheese tasting and fine dining interspersed with traditional Christian observances and displays of patriotism.

The merchant wanted to talk to Jesus to know if he was the real Messiah, the True God. If so, he hoped to show him the good work he was doing and to receive his blessing. He was filled with joy when Jesus and his apostles arrived in the luxurious hotel lobby.

The merchant led Jesus and the apostles on a tour of the conference, stopping first at the door of the main ballroom. It was filled with many well-dressed men and women listening to a cleric railing against abortion. The audience applauded his denunciations of abortion and evil pro-choice physicians. The merchant said to Jesus, "You see, it is as you have taught. Abortion is the worst of all evils. Nothing else even comes close in the attack on the sanctity of life." Jesus heard him and nodded but asked, "What about my poor brothers and sisters?"

The merchant ignored the question and led them to a conference room where preparations were being made for a Patriotic Distribution of the Holy Eucharist. The ritual was to honor the Conference's guest speaker, the nation's Secretary of Defense. The merchant bowed his head and made the sign of the cross. Jesus cast a doubtful look at the Apostles.

Finally the merchant led them to another conference room just in time to hear the closing words of the Pledge of Allegiance, "…one nation under God, indivisible, with liberty and justice for all." The merchant took Jesus aside and said to him, "Love of country is so important. Don't you agree?"

Jesus said to him in reply, "Follow me." And he led the merchant to the bar. He asked the bartender for the remote control, took it and clicked at the television. The image of the desiccated body of a migrant in the Sonora Desert appeared. With another click, images of skeletal, wide-eyed Sudanese children came up on the screen. With one more click Jesus showed the merchant images of food pantries closing their doors in the faces of impoverished Appalachian families. Jesus said to the merchant. "Do you not have eyes to see with? Do not these, the least of my brothers, also deserve the same concern as my unborn brothers? Have you not heard my teaching in the temple according to Isaiah? Feed the hungry. Clothe the naked. Release the oppressed from their burdens? Instead of wining and dining with your wealthy friends, seeking their admiration and praise, go sell your possessions and give to the poor. Only then should you go to your room, close the door and pray to Him in secret to forgive you. You have ignored my teachings. Repent or face the unquenchable fires of Gehenna!" And he led the Apostles from that place.

CHAPTER 14

The End is Near

"The kingdom of God cometh not with observation. Neither shall they say: Behold here, or behold there. For lo, the kingdom of God is within you."[64]

WALKING ACROSS THE WATERS OF the Potomac, Jesus and his disciples made their way to the Capitol, because he had been invited to speak to a Joint Session of Congress. By now his fame had spread from New England to Florida and from the Atlantic to the Pacific. At the very foot of the staircase of the Capitol, just minutes before he was to speak to a Joint Session of Congress, throngs of men and women from near and far away listened to him teach about the Kingdom of God.

---

64 Luke 17: 20-21 (D)

A paralytic carried by four men was brought to him in the huge crowd, strong in their faith that Jesus would cure their friend. They pushed desperately to get near Jesus. Jesus becalmed the people and told the men to place the paralyzed man at his feet. When he saw the man's faith, he said to him, "Young man, your sins are forgiven. Get up off that mat and go on home."[65] The man rose and left with his friends, leaping and jumping with joy and praising God.

There were many others that afternoon at the Capitol that threw aside their crutches, rose from their wheelchairs, saw with their eyes and heard with their ears for the first time. Several top medical CEOs who happened to be in town lobbying for their industry could not believe the wonders they saw. As they looked up in the sky, they saw a host of angels descending to carry Jesus in glory into the Capitol building. One of them murmured to the others, "How can we put a stop to this?"

Leaving the crowds and the angels behind, Jesus entered the Chamber of the House with Michael the Archangel leading the way. His Apostles followed several paces behind him. For the occasion, Jesus had his shepherd's

---

65 Cf. Mark, 2: 11-12 "I say to thee: Arise, take up they bed and go into thy house. And immediately he arose; and taking up his bed, went his way in the sight of all; so that all wondered and glorified God, saying: We never saw the like." (D)

staff and wore his traditional white robe and sandals. He proceeded to the podium amid loud cheers on both sides of the aisle. The four Apostles took seats reserved for them in the front row next to the Supreme Court Justices.

The eyes of the nation were upon Congress. C-Span was broadcasting the Joint Session. By this time, the country was swept with amazement because of the miracles and wonders Jesus had performed in recent days. Excitement over the Kingdom of God and what shape it would take was running high. Across the land many of the one-percent were dispirited. Wealthy people hid their treasure in secure bunkers. Some came forth and offered to pay their fair share of taxes. In remote areas, survivalists prepared for the apocalypse. People in the inner cities were euphoric, imagining the delights that awaited them. Some deplorable people went on a rampage but this was rare. Mostly, there was a good feeling in the air. Neighbors were friendlier. Charitable contributions were up. People greeted strangers cordially and they fed the hungry, clothed the naked and visited prisoners. Clearly there had been a paradigm shift and Congress was aware, like never before, of the nation's high expectations for change. It had taken the miracle of Jesus's Second Coming.

Jesus looked at both sides of the chamber and then he said to the legislators, "Sit and listen, those of you who have ears to hear with. I have come here, not to make peace, but to shake things up. I rebuke some of you for turning this House into a den of thieves.[66] You, men and women who have the best health insurance package in the land; you who keep the people you represent, especially the least of my brothers and sisters, from access to health care in your states; you, who consort only with millionaires and billionaires; you who lift not a finger to help widows recover their homes; you brood of vipers—you grow fat on bribes and emoluments while you plot to do away with aid to millions struggling to make a living. You demand that the least of my brothers 'tighten their belts,' and yet you increase tax breaks for the rich who fatten on corporate profits. Be ready, I say to you. My Kingdom is at hand. The least of my brothers will be first and you who are now first, will be last."

Some legislators cowered in silence. Some muttered under their breath that Jesus was a phony, a quack, yea, a charlatan and that they had seen him having lunch with bums and women who sinned. But Jesus knew what was in their hardened hearts. "I say to you, that bums, tax collectors and sinners all the lower classes—will enter the kingdom of God before you."[67]

---

66 Cf. Matthew, 21: 13 "It is written 'My house shall be called the house of prayer, but you have made it a den of thieves.'; John 2, 16 "Take these things hence, and make not the house of my Father a house of traffic."

67 Cf. "Matthew 21: 31 "Jesus saith to them: Amen I say to you, that the publicans and the harlots shall go into the kingdom of God before you."

Some senators began to protest. One of them stood and called out, "Liar! Anti-Christ!"

"Amen, I say. You are nothing but hypocrites. Pious do-gooders on the outside but full of malice and evil on the inside.[68] My Father in Heaven sees you! Woe to those who see and yet do not believe and to those who hear but do not listen. You will weep on the Day of Judgment

Those of you who show repentance I will receive into my house. Until the last minute, I offer you forgiveness and compassion.

The Kingdom of God is like a mansion with many rooms. And I am going to need many rooms! The challenge will be great to bring back all past generations in the Resurrection. And that will be just the beginning of my work! Sorting the sheep and the goats will be even more difficult and will require good judgment and time. Moreover, the rapture of all those billions into the Kingdom will require strategy and logistics. Don't expect it to happen overnight. So, when you ask where is the Kingdom of God, I will say, 'It's here. It's there. It's now. It will soon come to be.'

---

68 Based on Matthew, 23: 27-28 "Woe to you scribes and Pharisees, hypocrites; because you are like to whited sepulchers, which outwardly appear to men to be beautiful, but within are full of dead men's bones, and of all filthiness."

I have miraculous powers, of course. And I have legions of angels helping me. Nonetheless, there will be an interim between the Resurrection and the Rapture. And during that period I'll need your help here on earth. You must make the earth the staging ground for the Kingdom of God, keep my commandments above all and protect and nourish life here on land, on sea and in the air.

Whether you call yourself a Democrat, a Republican, a Socialist or an Independent matters not to me. You will all need to follow the basic rule of giving away most of your wealth and keeping only the minimum. This applies equally to your president whom I will see the day after tomorrow. Stay calm. Don't get too excited. Plan for the long term. With my miraculous powers, your cooperation, and with help from the angels we'll make it. I've got to go now. Thank you everyone. I bless you."

He raised his hand in blessing and left the stage, again led by Michael the Archangel who kept the aisle clear with his blazing sword. The Apostles fell in behind them.

The members of Congress stood, amazed. Some applauded, while others still doubted. Still others simply rejected the word of God.

Outside, at the foot of the steps of the Capitol, Simon-Peter called a cab. When they all piled in, he told the cabdriver to head for the town of Lynchburg, a town about one hundred eighty miles away in the center of the state of Virginia.

CHAPTER 15

The Good Samaritan

"Which of these three, in thy opinion, was neighbor to him that fell among the robbers?"[69]

ALL OF WASHINGTON, D.C. HAD heard about the strong warnings that Jesus had given the authorities. Marches and demonstrations in support of his address to Congress began immediately and swept across the country.

Jesus and the Apostles arrived at the small town of Lynchburg and found a large inn not far from Liberty University. He went there to rest before making a planned appearance before a gathering of white supremacists.

---

69 Luke, 10: 36 (D)

Jesus entered the large room where they were meeting and went to the stage. He said to them, "As I look around this room and see so many blond-haired, blue-eyed people, it makes me wonder. My Father and I created man in the image of God but we worked hard to introduce some superficial differences into the product, as you know. Do you realize that we developed fifty-seven different shades for human skin, for instance? Not to mention variations in hair, eyes, height, shape of teeth, ears, limbs, voice and so on. The idea was to create a pleasant variety while keeping the same basic model. You've heard the old saying, 'Variety is the spice of life' haven't you? We thought it would be a source of enjoyment for you to sit on your porches or look out your windows and see neighbors with different traits. If everyone in the world looked the same it would be boring. Or, so we thought. Things didn't work out as we expected, especially here, in this beautiful land of yours."

Some in the audience murmured against him, saying, "Who is this man who acts as if he is greater than the God of our fathers and who claims to have created mankind in his image?"

Jesus directed his words at hooded men in the front rows. "Whether or not our efforts were successful, it was always our intention that you should love one another. For the greatest commandment is to love God with your whole heart and to love your fellow man as much as you care for yourself. So why, you may ask, have I come here among you? Why now, at this late hour of your president's reign? It is because, if only for one brief moment before this world passes away, my Father and I would like to see some proof, some justification for our faith in the basic goodness of mankind."

Some men with shaved heads started mocking and hooting at him.

But Jesus said, "Listen to this story. It's about one of your fellow Klansmen, who was, in fact, a Grand Wizard by night and a gun salesman by day from Birmingham, Alabama. One day, as he was driving through the countryside on a remote road, his car broke down. He coasted to the side of the road, got out and raised the hood. Soon another car pulled up behind him. Two white men, each bigger than he, came over, one wielding a tire iron. They shoved him around, beat him with their fists and clubbed him, inflicting serious injuries. He slumped to the ground, propped up against the front bumper. They took a rifle from the trunk of the man's car; they cleaned out his wallet and threw it in a ditch. Then they took his watch, his shoes and even his outer garments. Then they drove off laughing, leaving him bloody, naked and semi-conscious."

Hecklers in the audience settled down and listened without interruption as Jesus continued with his parable. "The poor, bloodied Klansman waved to attract the attention of passersby on the country road. But the cars kept going. After ten minutes of waving, he saw one car slow down to a crawl. Its driver was a white man. This man saw your comrade but he sped up and left the scene. The Klansman despaired of getting any help in his distress until another car slowed down. This time it was a clergyman at the wheel and the Grand Wizard rejoiced. But, like the previous gawker, the clergyman took a brief look and drove off. He was a Christian clergyman, I tell you, and a white man at that! Your brother almost lost consciousness at that point. Now, a third man drove up, stopped his car and actually got out. He looked around cautiously before approaching the victim because he was black and feared being shot without cause by the authorities.

The Klansman, too, feared it was certain death for him. But instead of killing him, the black man tended to his needs and got him into his own car. Minutes later, he pulled into a farmyard in front of a little house and dropped him off. That was the last time he saw his rescuer before he passed out.

Two days later, he awoke in a plain but tidy bedroom, looking into the faces of two wide-eyed little black girls. His arms, face and chest were bandaged. The girls fled from the room, calling for their mother who led them by the hand back into the room. 'How did I get here?' the Klansman asked the woman. 'A man brought you here. He gave me money to use for your care. He said he would come back soon and give me as much money as necessary to get you back on your feet. You better just rest some more. I'll bring you something to eat.' As she turned to leave, she said, 'The man who found you also found your wallet. There was a card inside that says you're a Grand Wizard. So, I know. But you can relax. You have nothing to fear from my little girls and me.'"

When he finished saying these things to the Klansmen in the packed hall, Jesus asked, "Which of the three drivers was the righteous one?"

The audience was silent. At last, one of the cone-hatted men in the front row stood and said in reply, "The nigger was the righteous one, hate to say it."

Jesus nodded, "The third man was righteous and he will have everlasting life. Therefore, I tell you, go and do likewise. And lose those silly sheets, men."

That day many came forward, seeking Jesus's blessing and glorifying God's name. And just as many refused to repent.

Jesus said to these, "Woe unto you. Tomorrow, unless you repent, my angels will take you down to Gehenna where you will receive the same punishment that you meted out to the righteous. Be gone, you accursed ones!" Then he went upstairs to his room at the inn and planned for the next day's meeting with the President in Washington.

CHAPTER 16

This World Shall Pass

THE ARCHANGEL MICHAEL, BRANDISHING HIS flaming sword, escorted Jesus to the Oval Office of the White House for a private meeting with the President. The President welcomed Jesus and gestured to a seat. "Welcome, welcome, Jesus. Or should I call you Your Holiness or something like that?

He said in reply, "Call me Master. I am the Master of this house now."

The President smiled, thinking Jesus was just a popular, but somewhat unbalanced, guru. He did not yet understand who Jesus really was. He said to Jesus, "Thank you, yes. Well, have a seat. To be honest, it's a feather in my cap to have you here today. You know, a month ago I had the Dalai Lama in for a visit, too. I wish I could get him to be my Press Secretary or something. The real deal, I gotta tell you. I got so much favorable publicity from his visit. So much. And just last week I had the Pope in for a quick visit. Nice man. Very nice man. Very, very nice. So nice. You know what I mean? A little pontificating, though."

"Your meaning is very clear. You reject the prophets."

The President ignored this and continued the banter. "So, I've heard so much about you on TV. Miracles in Boston and D.C., great big crowds everywhere you go. New York, Baltimore. That was amazing. Reminds me of my campaign days. And those healings you do at every stop on the road. I can't get over it. How do you do that?"

"It's not I who do them, but my Father. He sent me and I do his will on earth, the same as in Heaven. We are together on everything."

"Your dad must be great. Give him my regards next time you see him. I got to say, you're so popular. Big league."

Jesus tired of the small talk. "Let's get down to business. What have you done to help the least of my brothers?"

The President stiffened. "Well, a lot, in fact. I may be a billionaire but I'm all for the little guy. And I notice you've been very tough on my wealthy friends on your tour. Seems like you're often pointing the blame at us. So unfair. So, so unfair."

"That's not the point. You've been chosen to lead the nation under Me, with liberty and justice for all. So, once more, what exactly have you done for the poor?"

"I've reduced taxes on business, removed all kinds of idiotic regulations and I've made more millionaires than this country has ever seen before. And I've put lots of them in charge. That's how I've kept my promise to the American people. You satisfied?"

Jesus cast him a baleful look and said, "Look, I have no special admiration for the wealthy. They're no better than anyone else. I'm going to talk straight with you."

"Good," the President said with a broad smile. "That's what I expect. Shoot."

Jesus told him, "The correct answer to my question is that you have done nothing for the poor. Nothing. You can't point to a single blessed thing you've done for the least of my brothers and sisters. And you don't have any plans in that direction either. You are also leading some of my sheep astray. So, the three of us on the Board have decided to remove you as of right now."

The smile left the President's face. "What Board?

Jesus said to him, "Me, my Father and the Holy Spirit. The Holy Trinity. Do you not yet understand who I am? We are the Board and our Kingdom is at hand. Be gone, evil-doer!"

The President was shocked and replied, "What the…? You act like you're God. You're ridiculous. Who the hell are you, anyway?"

"I Am God. And I'm talking to you."[70]

The President shouted, "Get outta here! Loser!" For even yet he did not understand.

Jesus groaned, "You know what? You're really getting to me." He was about to call in the Archangel Michael to haul him off, but paused. "What on earth am I going to do with you?" he mumbled, shaking his head woefully. "I thought this was going to be easy—just walk in and get it over with."

He stood at the windows behind the President's desk, staring out and pondering aloud. "You can't be right in the head!

---

70 Cf. John: 4: 26 "I am he, the one who is speaking with thee." (D)

That has to be the problem. You claim to be a champion of everyday people while you crow about your money. You surround yourself with millionaires and billionaires—the better to feather your nest and theirs. You reduce medical care to those most in need while you throw money at arms merchants. Woe unto you!" Jesus raised his eyes to Heaven and said, "I've had enough of it. Father, what am I going to do with this confused sinner?"

A voice thundered overhead, "Son, forgive him, for he knows not what he does. Something is sadly missing at the core. He's just not up to the job. I'm confident you'll figure something out. Don't give up yet on the miscreant."

Jesus paused for a minute. Then he said to the President, "My Father is right. You're in over your head. It should never have come to this." Just then, Michael the Archangel came in and asked Jesus what the delay was all about. The Gehenna Express was waiting out at the north portico, he said, waving his flaming sword impatiently. Jesus told him to wait a second. He was dealing with a troublesome case.

Jesus said to the President, "I have an idea. I think I have just the right job for you in the Kingdom of Heaven. Thing is, you'll have to repent before I give you this plum of a job."

At the sight of Archangel Michael with his flaming sword, the President trembled, for at last he understood that he could not put one over on Jesus. And he realized he might soon be climbing on board the express to Hell.

Jesus asked, "Well, do you repent?"

"Yes, sir. Yes, I do. Your dad's one hundred percent correct. Please forgive me for I not know what I do. I mean I know not what I do."

"You sure of that?"

"I'm sure as hell."

"Very well. I say unto you, sell all your assets."

"No blind trust?"

"No! With you, trust is not the word that first comes to mind. You will order your assets to be distributed to the least of my brothers and sisters around the world. When you have done that, go to this address and ask for a job." And Jesus handed him a business card with the address of the Good Shepherd Mission House in Baltimore. "Be quick about it. There's a burning need for volunteers in the soup kitchen. Remember, I'll be watching you, so don't try to pull anything sneaky." At that, the Archangel Michael pointed his fiery sword at the door and ordered the President out of the Oval Office.

Epilogue

THE FIRST DAY AFTER THE President found work at the Good Shepherd Mission House, Jesus instituted the Kingdom of God in America.

On the second day, the Kingdom spread to all parts of the Americas, Europe, Asia, Africa, the Atlantic and the Pacific, East and West, North and South.

On the third day, billionaires fled from office and were instantly replaced by men and women acclaimed by the people. They ruled with the welfare of the people in mind, not the interests of the selfish and power-hungry few. The separation of the righteous from the wicked got under way. And for once, the last got priority while the first went to the back of the line.

On the fourth day, American individuals and corporate persons paid their taxes in a way that was commensurate with their income. The jobless found work with wages that would support their families. The sick received good medical attention. The homeless found housing and immigrants and refugees were welcomed with open arms at borders around the world. Those imprisoned for political reasons or trivial offenses were released. The mentally ill and the downcast received proper attention. The world received a peace dividend as swords were beaten into plowshares and the merchants of death went out of business.

On the fifth day, Jesus attended to the natural world and its long history of despoliation. Community organizations and benevolent brotherhoods helped neighborhoods, towns and cities to clean up. Regional governments hired workers to restore forests, rivers, and seacoasts. Nations reformed agriculture to make the soil and crops healthy again and worked with each other to end all forms of environmental poisoning and the threat of nuclear war.

On the sixth day, Jesus called forth all past generations in the great Resurrection, all the while uplifting the lowly and reducing the proud, continuing the task of sorting the sheep from the goats and preparing for the day of Glory.

On the seventh day, Jesus, his Father and the Holy Spirit looked upon their work and said, "This is good." Then, the three of them headed out for a short vacation on a tropical island.

BIBLICAL REFERENCES AND EXCERPTS IN this story are based on the Douay-Rheims Bible, translated from St. Jerome's Latin Vulgate. On the website, BestCatholicBible.com., it is described as the "safest, most traditional and most trustworthy Catholic Bible" The website also describes it as more majestic and poetic than other modern translations.

I also consulted The New American Bible, copyright 1987 by Devore and Sons, Wichita, Kansas. This translation makes use of a more contemporary idiom and eschews the stately, archaic style found in the Douay-Rheims version. For the convenience of the reader I have signaled the use of the Douay version in the footnotes with (D) and the New American Bible with (A)

Undoubtedly, in the short time that Jesus spent 'on the road' teaching the good news, he lavished his great concern and compassion on those considered to be out-castes or lowly. Today, Jesus would show particular attention to broad swaths of the population labeled 'the disadvantaged,' 'low income earners' or the 'homeless' in addition to the imprisoned, the sick at all levels of society, the handicapped, the lonely and neglected and, of course refugees and immigrants. He would also have strong advice for this generation's so-called one percent. Christianity calls for more than faith in Jesus; it demands performance of good works, following his clear and insistent example.

The present era in America is almost without parallel for the scope and magnitude of grasping and greed. It makes the Belle Epoque of the late 19th century look a bit threadbare by comparison. The everyday American is aware of the economic injustice both from the stagnation in his wages over the past four decades and from hearing the giant sucking sound of profits whooshing to the uppermost, thinnest stratum of society. Besides wage stagnation, another contributor to the average American's plight is wage theft that takes many forms. One reporter has written about a scandal in Italy that certainly has its counterpart in the United States. Responding to this kind of scandal, the Pope expressed his anger at the hypocrisy of a company owner who professed to be Catholic and who withheld wages from his employees even while he went off on grand vacations in the eastern Mediterranean.[71]

The intent of *Jesus in America, Miracles and Parables of His Second Coming* is to focus the reader's attention on the critical core message of the Christian Gospels, i.e., the Kingdom of God and love of God and one's fellow man. It also shines a light on areas in contemporary American society and politics that appear sharply, if not altogether hypocritically, opposed to that message. It does so by a combination of new tales and direct quotations from sacred text, in particular, statements by Jesus, miracles he performed and parables he told. In telling this story, the author believes that the Jesus of the Gospels is clearly recognizable here by his uncompromising condemnation of greed and his boundless concern for the excluded.

71 Doug Stranglin, USA Today, February 24, 2017, "Pope Takes on Catholics Who Lead a Double Life."

About the Author

BRANDON PHILIPS IS FROM A large Irish family. He has taught in California for many years. He and his wife make their home in Hawaii.

THE EMPRESS RUBY: AN ACTION adventure that pits decorated war hero and U.S. Marine, Mike Morales, and his friends against a corrupt President and his ambitions First Lady. It's the eve of the Presidential Election of 2024 and the American Republic is teetering on the edge of civil collapse. Can Corporal Morales and his friends save the nation from a takeover by greedy corporate lords and their media mouthpieces? Fast-paced and action-packed, the Morales's mission plays out across Asia, America and Europe.

Gold of the Khan: Brace yourself for a wild adventure that whisks you across the globe in search of the legendary treasure of Kublai Khan. Marya Bradwell, Harvard professor of History, sets out to unlock the mystery of its whereabouts. In so doing, she encounters Liam Di Angelo, a shady antiquities dealer, and clashes with him over priceless pieces that once belonged to Kublai Khan and Marco Polo. She and

Di Angelo both run afoul of a sadistic, self-styled Khan and are about to learn that they are on to a high-stakes secret that will rock China and Russia to their foundations! In a dangerous game of terror and greed can she trust anyone with the clues that only she holds?

Losing Ground: The Displacement of San Gorgonio Pass Cahuilla People in the 19th Century: Winner of the American Association of State and Local History Award for Leadership in History. Co-authored with Louis Doody and Betty Kikumi Meltzer. Highly acclaimed and used in college courses, **Losing Ground** reveals a hidden chapter of American history—the dependence of white settlers on Native American labor in the early years of the American takeover of California and the near elimination of these first people from their Southern California homelands. Be sure to see Losing Ground's companion book for younger readers, ***Glimpses of History, The San Gorgonio Pass in the 19th Century.***